The Big Book of
Football Stories

The Big Book of
Football Stories

Published by the Penguin Group
Penguin Books Ltd, 27 Wrights Lane, London W8 5TZ, England
Penguin Putnam Inc., 375 Hudson Street, New York, New York 10014, USA
Penguin Books Australia Ltd, Ringwood, Victoria, Australia
Penguin Books Canada Ltd, 10 Alcorn Avenue, Toronto, Ontario, Canada M4V 3B2
Penguin Books (NZ) Ltd, Private Bag 102902, NSMC, Auckland, New Zealand

On the World Wide Web at: *www.penguin.com*

Penguin Books Ltd, Registered Offices: Harmondsworth, Middlesex, England

Why We Got Chucked Out of the Inter-Schools Football Competition first published by
Hamish Hamilton Ltd 1995; published in Puffin Books 1996

How We Got Back into the Inter-Schools Football Competition
first published in Puffin Books 1998

Milly of the Rovers first published by Viking 1996; published in Puffin Books 1998

This edition published by Viking 2000
1 3 5 7 9 10 8 6 4 2

Why We Got Chucked Out of the Inter-Schools Football Competition
text copyright © David Ross, 1995
Why We Got Chucked Out of the Inter-Schools Football Competition
illustrations copyright © Jacqui Thomas, 1995
How We Got Back into the Inter-Schools Football Competition
text copyright © David Ross, 1998
How We Got Back into the Inter-Schools Football Competition
illustrations copyright © Jacqui Thomas, 1998
Milly of the Rovers text copyright © Harriet Castor, 1996
Milly of the Rovers illustrations copyright © Christyan Fox, 1996
All rights reserved

The moral right of the authors and illustrators has been asserted

Printed and bound in Great Britain by The Bath Press

British Library Cataloguing in Publication Data
A CIP catalogue record for this book is available from the British Library

ISBN 0-670-89358-7

Contents

Why We Got Chucked Out
of the Inter-Schools Football
Competition   1

How We Got Back into the
Inter-Schools Football
Competition   95

Milly of the Rovers   191

DAVID ROSS

Why we got chucked out of The Inter-Schools Football Competition

Illustrated by Jacqui Thomas

For William

1. *The Goalkeeper (Ashton Jackson)*

IT'S EASY FOR some people to criticise, isn't it? Blame the goalie. But our side only had to score more goals than the other lot did, and we'd have won. But we didn't score any goals at all. And I let in – well, I'll tell you later, after I've explained a bit more.

I have to admit, I wasn't feeling all that well. I don't even like playing football. It makes me nervous, with this big, heavy ball flying around. I might get hurt, and when I think about that, I get short of breath. When I get short of breath, I have to lie down. But you can't lie down in the goal mouth.

I didn't do any training for the match; there wasn't time. I didn't know until the day before that I was playing. I'm the reserve goalkeeper for the Skimpole Street School First Eleven (First and Only – there isn't another team). The regular keeper is Piano Legs Cooper. It was when he got chickenpox that they got on to me. Sarvindar Patel, he's the captain, said, "Jackson, you're on. You're the goalie tomorrow, against Stapleton Road."

"What?" I said. "You're kidding."

"I wish I was," said Patel. "We need you. Piano Legs is sick."

Piano Legs is never sick. He's the healthiest person I know. He's horribly healthy. That's why I've never kept goal before. I thought I was quite safe being the reserve keeper, sort of in the football team without having to play. It started just because once, long ago, they were playing football in the playground. I wasn't playing; I was having an argument with Margery O'Neil about whether miles were longer than kilometres. She thinks they're not. All of a sudden I heard a shout:

"Ashton, look out!"

I was standing right in front of the big window of the canteen. The ball came zooming down at me out of the sky. Without even thinking, I jumped up and caught it, with my eyes shut.

"Oof!" It knocked all the breath out of me, and I sat down very hard, still holding the ball. Everyone was very surprised, and Sarvindar, who was the one that kicked it up so high, was very pleased.

"It would have broken the window, for sure," he said. "You're a natural goalie, Jackson. Who'd have thought it, a wimp like you?"

"It was a fluke," said someone else.

"No, he's got fantastic reflexes. He could be an ace goalie."

"Well done, Wimpy," they all said. I didn't say I grabbed it just to stop it hitting me in the face. Ever since then,

I've been the reserve keeper for the school team.

My mum didn't want me to play. She said I was looking pale, and she took my temperature, but it turned out to be normal.

"I don't trust this thermometer," she said. "You don't look normal to me. I'm going to buy another one. And it's a nasty, raw-looking day. It won't do your chest any good, standing in goal for an hour and a half. Perhaps you'd better stay at home."

I wish now I hadn't argued. But I said, "Aw, Mum, I'll be all right. And they haven't anyone else; I can't let the team down."

The truth is, I was feeling rather pleased to have been chosen. How could I have known how awful it would be?

In the end my mum gave my chest a good rub with Super-Strong

Embrocation and made me wear a woolly winter vest, but she let me go.

I had to wear Piano Legs' kit. As he's about twice my weight, it didn't fit very well. I had to tie the shorts up with string, and if I lifted my feet off the ground too quickly, the boots fell off. That didn't exactly help.

I did try to keep goal properly in the match with Stapleton Road. But somehow, I never quite got to the ball. When I jumped, I didn't jump high enough, because I was too busy curling my toes into the boots and holding on to the shorts with one hand to stop the string slipping. When the ball came low, I never got there in time. Well, I don't like throwing myself on to hard, muddy ground. And sometimes it came really fast and I thought it might sting my hands. Once I did catch it, and was so surprised that I let it drop again, over the line.

"I don't believe it," said our captain.

"Well, keep them away," I said. "Go and score some goals up at the other end."

"Sixteen-nil," he said. "And it's not

even half-time yet."

When it all came to an end, the score was twenty-two to nil. I don't think I'll be asked to keep goal again. Sarvindar Patel was quite rude.

"I'd sooner have your granny keeping goal than you," he said afterwards. "You never even got dirty." He and the others had got covered in mud. There was a long

skid-mark in the mud to one side of
our goal where he had slid along,
trying to get the ball away from the
Stapleton Road striker. I don't know
what my mum would say if she saw me
like that.

"My hands were dirty," I said.

"Huh, from picking up the ball after
they scored," said Patel.

Well, I don't care. I never asked to
be the goalkeeper. The game I really
like is tiddlywinks. I can beat anybody
at that.

2. *The First Defender*
(Kevin Brown)

I DIDN'T START the fight. It's always my brother who starts things.

"You take it," he shouts to me, when that big tall Stapleton Roader comes running up with the ball.

"No, you," I say back. "I'm marking the winger, can't you see?"

So the Stapleton Roader comes right through the middle, with Patel yelling, "Stop him, you idiots!" and slams the ball past Wimpy, who runs away in the other direction. The ref blows his whistle. Another goal to them.

"Why didn't you stop him, like I

told you to?" says Norman. He's my brother. My twin brother. Twenty minutes older, so he thinks he's the boss.

"He was yours," I say. "I had to mark that winger. If he'd passed the ball to him, we'd have been left wide open. You should have tackled."

"He was over on your side."

"No he wasn't."

"Yes he was."

"Anyway, you're not the skipper. I don't have to take orders from you."

"Well, if you'd done what I said, we might have saved that goal. You never listen, do you?"

"I don't need any orders from you."

"Both of you have to run more," says Patel. "You have to cover the centre as well as the wings."

Then it's kick-off again, and,

unbelievably, the ball gets into their
half. It's hardly been there at all so far
in the match. They've been all over us.
Little Patel is up there, so are Jones,
Gibson, Anderson, all the rest of them;
everyone except Norman, me and
Wimpy Jackson.

"Go on, Skimpole, score!" I shout.

But out comes the ball with the tall
player again. He can run like anything,
taking the ball with him as if it was
part of his boot. I can hear Patel
shouting. I've got to stop him. I will
stop him. I can hear shouting but I'm
not listening, I'm concentrating on
taking the ball from the Stapleton
Roader. Then suddenly there's a huge
thump, and I'm knocked sideways and
fall flat in the cold, muddy grass. My
idiot brother has run right into me.

"You fool," I try to shout, but I

haven't enough breath. He's sitting on the ground too, glaring at me. He's got no puff either, but I can see his lips move, saying something nasty. A cry goes up from the Stapleton Road side. Lanky Long-legs has scored again. Poor Wimpy has picked up the ball and is holding it as if it's a bomb about to go off.

"He was mine," says my brother at last.

"No he wasn't. I was nearer."

"Didn't you hear me? I said to leave it."

I can feel my ribs aching where he collided with me.

."You pushed me."

"No, I didn't."

"You did. You put your fist right in my ribs."

"I was just trying to keep my balance."

"Liar."

"Don't call me a liar."

"Yah, liar."

"You're the liar."

"Rotten stinking liar. And you can't play football."

"That's another lie."

Okay, I suppose I did hit him first.

But he was asking for it. Even before
the football match. He'd been getting
on my nerves all morning. He took
three Weetabix out of the packet at
breakfast and only left two for me. And
he took most of the milk. And he eats
my peanut butter. Our mum started
getting the two kinds, crunchy for him
and smooth for me, because nasty
Norman says he doesn't like the
smooth kind. But today my jar was
nearly empty, and I know why. He's
decided he prefers the smooth sort
after all, and he's been sneaking it. He
thinks I don't know, but I do. I always
know what he's up to.

So I hit him, sort of, in the ribs, and
he hit me back, right on my sore ear.
He knew I had a sore ear, because I
told him. He just laughed, though.
Then later, he hits me on it. That's the

sort of brother I've got. I knocked him over into the mud, but he pulled me down with him, and I ended up underneath. By the time the ref had pulled us apart, we were covered in mud. He had a black eye, and I had a big lump on my lip. And my sore ear was really aching. I accidentally sort of caught the referee's leg with my boot as he dragged us up, and he got really wild.

"Off," he said. "Both of you. What do you think you are? Professionals?"

He was in a bad temper already, and that was before the dog came on the pitch and bit a hole in his shorts. So Skimpole Street was two men down, and it wasn't even half-time. Wimpy Jackson watched us going.

"What do I do now?" he wailed.

"Go home," said Norman.

3. The Captain
(Sarvindar Patel)

WHAT A NIGHTMARE! I'd sooner walk
the tightrope over a tank full of
piranha fish than go through that
again. My first time as captain, and we
lose the first game twenty-two to
nothing. In the first half. Not only
that, we get disqualified from the
competition. I'm not sure what was the
exact reason for us being thrown out.
Those stupid Browns didn't help. The
dog didn't help. Charlie Gibson's
injury probably didn't make much
difference. But Gary Sandford's
mother didn't help. And what

happened at half-time just put the lid on everything.

There had been problems from the very start.

The Head, Mr Watkins, got very excited. He's always excited about something. He comes from Wales and has bright red hair that sticks out over his ears. When he's really excited, his face gets very pink and his eyes look as if they're going to pop out.

"Patel, my boy, I'm making you captain of the First Eleven for the Inter-Schools Football Competition. You'll have the best turned-out team in the whole tournament," he said to me. "I've arranged with the Ghengis Khan Fast Food Takeaway to provide a new strip. Mr Abdullah was delighted to be asked. All he wants in return is for young Abdullah to be

included in the team. That's all right,
isn't it, Patel? You can fit him in
somewhere, can't you?"

"Aw, sir," I said. "Abdullah's
useless. He's too fat. He can't run. He
can't even see his feet – "

"Now, Patel, that's enough. We'll have no fat-ism in Skimpole Street School. Young Bayram Abdullah may have a weight problem, but that's no reason to leave him out of the football team. It may give him just the right sort of encouragement to try to slim down a bit."

"But, sir, he can't play football."

"Well, he's only one, isn't he? You have nine others in the side, plus yourself. And the new kit I've got for you should be a terrific boost for the team. It's worth having young Abdullah in it just for that. I've got a feeling that Skimpole Street will come out on top this time, for once. Now run along, and stop making difficulties. Think Positive, Patel!"

Mr Watkins doesn't like being contradicted. He always Thinks

Positive. I think that Thinking Positive just means agreeing with Mr Watkins.

It was all right in our training sessions. We had some good people in the team. Laurence Murphy is brilliant in midfield, and Piano Legs Cooper is a really good goalkeeper. And some of the others aren't too bad, including me. The Brown twins are okay when they aren't fighting. And even if he's only got one leg, old Mr Hitchin knows a lot about football. It's a pity his memory isn't what it was. He's our trainer, because we haven't had a PT teacher at Skimpole Street School since Mr Rumbold pulled the wallbars down on top of himself and broke his legs.

It wasn't his fault. He didn't know they had been unfixed so that the wall behind could be painted. Mr Watkins should have told him, but he was thinking about something else at the time, and forgot.

He did go to visit Mr Rumbold in hospital. We all signed a card for Mr Watkins to take along. But Mr Rumbold tried to throw a vase of flowers at him, which wasn't easy with two legs in plaster. He fell out of bed and broke his arm, which was just about the only thing that wasn't broken already.

So Mr Hitchin stepped into the gap as trainer. He's Sandford's grandfather. He was once considered for Tranmere Rovers when he was young, before he lost his leg. He can still get up quite a speed along the sidelines in his wheelchair. His special combination tactic was going to be our secret weapon.

"Get this right, and you're unbeatable," he said to me. "Now, just let me think. What was it? Was it 4-4-2? or 5-3-2?"

He took off his woolly hat and scratched his bald head.

"Let's see, now. The centre-forward takes the ball, and he passes it to his left. No, his right. Or is it? Well, he passes it and moves ahead to the twenty-yard line. The inside right is there to dummy, to make the defence think he's going to take the ball from the centre-half. But instead the centre-forward moves to the right, no, the left, and the centre-half passes the ball to him. Now comes the clever bit. They all think he's going to try for goal, but he passes it to the winger – "

"Which winger, Mr Hitchin?"

"What? Oh, just let me think a minute, until I get it straightened out in my mind."

I never did quite get the hang of it.
And then, two days before, Murpho
fell off his bike and sprained his ankle.
And Piano Legs got chicken pox.
Things began to look a bit bad. I
admit it was a mistake to pick Wimpy
Jackson for goal. And I shouldn't have
paired the Browns in defence. I accept
responsibility for that. But I couldn't
help the dog, or Sandford's mother, or
what happened at half-time. You can't
blame the captain for absolutely
everything.

Then there was the new strip. It was
horrible. Sort of slithery nylon stuff
that crackled when you touched it. The
shirts were bright yellow. The shorts
were bright green.

"Hee hee, look, a bunch of
daffodils," said someone from
Stapleton Road when we came out on

the pitch, and they all laughed. The shirts had G-K Takeaway – Fastest Food in Town in big letters on the back, and Skimpole Street School in very little letters on the front. I was glad the pitch was so muddy, it meant that soon we were all just mud-coloured.

I could see they had done more training than we had. We hardly got to touch the ball. Their PT teacher was there, a little bony man with a frizzy beard, who kept on jumping up from his bench and shouting things like, "Well done, Hognose!" or "Tackle closer, Fruitbat!" Maybe they weren't called Hognose and Fruitbat, but it sounded like it.

Old Mr Hitchin got very cross, and ran his wheelchair over the other trainer's foot just as he was getting up.

He said it was an accident, though the man with the beard said it was common assault and he was going to sue for damages. After that he could only hop about on one leg when he wanted to shout something.

When the dog came on, we were all down at our end. They had just scored their sixteenth goal, and the Brown twins had been sent off for fighting each other.

I knew the dog as soon as I saw it. It was Pongo, the big Dalmatian from the Green Dragon pub. It's just down the road from my dad's office. He's a friendly dog usually. I don't know why he bit the referee. He likes chewing things like old boots, not people.

The ref was out by himself in mid-field, and Pongo went straight for him. He only bit a piece out of the referee's shorts, really, but Mr Davis was very angry. He went quite pale. He and Mr Micklewell, Pongo's owner, had a loud argument.

"He was just being friendly," said

Mr Micklewell. "He's a great big puppy really. He'd never have harmed you."

"He's a menace," shouted Mr Davis, keeping a hand over his bottom. "You set him on to me deliberately. I heard you say 'Go for him, boy.' I shall report it. You won't get away with this."

"I didn't," said Mr Micklewell. "I was just shouting to the lads. I said 'Go for it, boys' not 'Go for him, boy'. Pongo just got a bit excited."

"I heard what I heard," said Mr Davis. "Intimidating the referee is a serious offence."

"I'm sorry," said Mr Micklewell. "It was an accident. Perhaps I can pay for a replacement pair of shorts."

"I shall make a full claim for

damages through the proper channels," said Mr Davis. "Luckily I brought a spare kit with me, or the game would have to be abandoned."

He tried to twist round to look at his bottom.

"I'm not sure he hasn't grazed the flesh, you know."

"Let me have a look," said Mr Micklewell, but Mr Davis quickly turned round the other way.

"That won't be necessary," he said. "The game is temporarily suspended while I retire to the pavilion."

He started back to the pavilion, walking backwards away from us. Mr

Micklewell went with him, still trying to explain that Pongo was friendly. I wonder if the ref knew that Mr Micklewell was Kevin and Norman Brown's uncle. Probably not, or he'd have been even more sure it wasn't an accident. After a long time, Mr Davis came out in a fresh kit, and blew his whistle for the game to start again.

And then we did get a chance, at last. Through Bayram Abdullah, of all people. He was fouled, inside the penalty area. He was just wandering about up there, when I got a lucky break. One of their forwards slipped and fell when he was on the ball, and it bounced over to me. I gave it a mighty kick upfield and went tearing after it. There was no one there but Bayram. Luckily he wasn't offside. There were two Stapleton Roaders between him and the goal.

"Get it, Bayram," I shouted. "Boot it in."

But poor Bayram can't move too fast, on account of being so fat. He started to go for the ball, but one of the defenders got there first. Say what you like about Bayram, he's really keen.

He came wallowing along and tried to get the ball, but the other boy pushed him off. The ref saw it, and awarded a penalty.

Laurence Murphy normally takes the penalty shots. But he wasn't there.

Suddenly you find the whole world shrinks to twelve yards of muddy grass and a goal-mouth. The Stapleton Road keeper was in front of me. He hadn't had much to do, so far, but he looked as if he knew his job.

I knew exactly where I was going to put the ball. Smack in the top left-hand corner of the net. That goalie wouldn't even see it go past him. I can kick the ball really hard. I nearly broke the big canteen window at school once with a kick from right across the playing field, but luckily Wimpy Jackson stopped it.

Anyway, I gave this one everything I'd got. Maybe I was too keen. I overdid it. I hit the ball just too low. It flew up into the air, clearing the bar by inches, kept on climbing, and disappeared over the fence behind the goal posts. There was a sound of

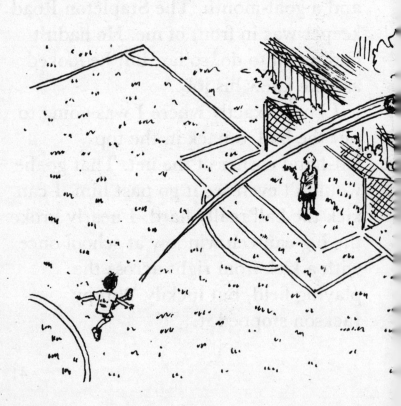

breaking glass. On the other side of the fence is the Willoughby Street allotments, with lots of little greenhouses.

I wanted to cry. But the captain can't cry.

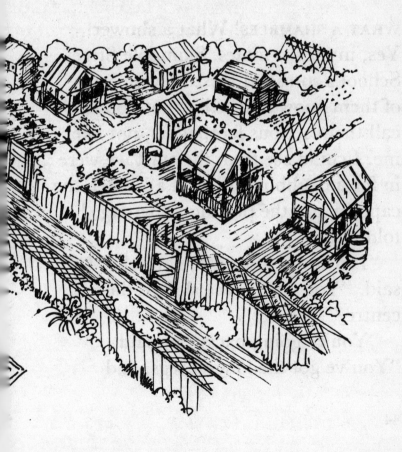

4. *The Player as Artist (Charlie Gibson)*

WHAT A SHAMBLES! What a shower!
Yes, my team-mates, Skimpole Street
School's so-called First Eleven. Some
of them know a little bit, but you can't
call them serious footballers, not like
me. I could see from the start we were
in for a drubbing. First of all Patel, the
captain, got the placing all wrong. I
told him.

"I'm ready to lead the attack," I
said. "You need some skill in the
centre."

"You're going back," he said.
"You've got the longest legs, and

we need a sweeper."

It's not that I want to be skipper myself. I could be, of course, but I'm basically a loner. There's an International player I model myself on, he's just my type – well, you'd only have to see me play to realise who I mean. We're so similar, it's amazing. I'm surprised that people don't seem to notice. It's a question of style. Brilliant, yes; good to watch, yes; temperamental, maybe, but with a right to be. When you're as good as that, you need things to be just right, and if they're not, then you owe it to yourself to complain.

Too many things that day weren't right for me. The weather for a start. Cold, windy, then it started to rain. I think I'll probably sign for an Italian club later, when I've turned professional. They have better weather there. Then to be stuck as a sweeper. No wonder I was seriously off form. Treating me as just another team player just isn't the way to get the best out of me. I need space to show my talent, out in front, leading the attack.

And the other side, Stapleton Road School, weren't the right sort of opposition. Don't get me wrong, I know that possession is the name of the game, but I'm not a physical player. Artistry is what I have – ball control, placing a lob just in the right spot, the well-timed header. But when these forwards just come crashing through, with their trainer howling at them to tackle, there's no chance. I don't know how many times I had the ball at my toe, and I was just about to make a perfect cross, the sort that makes the crowd gasp, when wham! they're on top of me, and the ball's gone.

Do you know what Patel shouted at me? "Get stuck in!" he said. There I was, doing my utmost, placed by him in completely the wrong position, unable to show my true skills, and all he could do was criticise.

No wonder I got cramp. At least it could have been the start of cramp. There was a definite feeling of something about to seize up. I knew it could come on any minute.

No one can say I didn't go out bravely. There was a throw-in, and their big forward came running out, punting the ball along in front of him. Talk about getting stuck in! I went for the ball like a tiger, but then thought my cramp might be coming on, so I gave a cry, started to hobble, then fell right in the mud, holding my leg. It was a beautiful fall, as good as any I've ever seen on TV.

"Aaah, cramp!" I gasped. "Just when I was about to get the ball. It's no good. I'll have to go off. Blast it."

"Sure, Charlie," said Patel, as if he couldn't care less. No thanks, no

sympathy. His star player cut down through no fault of my own, and he couldn't give a hoot. I did a specially big limp coming off the field, just to let him know. I went to the pavilion to rest and get some of Abdullah's half-time grub. I wish I hadn't stayed. Talk about being sick as a parrot.

5. *The Mother*
(Mrs Carrie Sandford)

HONESTLY, THAT REFEREE! What a fuss.
I don't see why he couldn't have
accepted me as a substitute. There was
poor old Skimpole Street, only eight
players on the field, being hopelessly
beaten by Stapleton Road. All these
Stapleton boys looked bigger, too.
Maybe they've been adding things to
their food in the school canteen, like
those athletes you hear about. They're
a funny lot up there at Stapleton.

Anyway, I was going to Safeways,
with little Gavin in his pushchair,
when I thought I'd look in at

Willoughby Park and see how Gary's football team was getting on. My Gary should be the captain, really. He'd be a very good captain. But Mr Watkins made that little Patel boy the captain, don't ask me why. You can have your guess and I'll have mine. Even when

Gary's grandpa went to all that trouble to be trainer, his own grandson couldn't be captain. Is that fair?

"What's the score, Dad?" I asked. I could see it wasn't going well. He looked as if he needed one of his purple pills to calm him down.

"Seventeen-nil," he said. "It's not a football match. It's the Battle of Waterloo."

Then that terrible little show-off

Charlie Gibson went off with cramp. At least he was saying he had cramp. There were only eight of them left. I think I decided there and then. But I waited for a while.

"Come on, Skimpole Street!" I shouted. "Come on, Gary!" It was hopeless. Even as I stood there, they scored again. I could see my Gary struggling bravely. Then I saw him being elbowed aside by a long, skinny boy when he tried to get at the ball.

"Hey, ref," I called out. "Have you got your eyes in your bottom? How much are the other side paying you?"

Fair comment, wouldn't you say? But he gave me a nasty, cold look.

"It's no good, Dad," I said. "I can't stand this. I'd sooner go on myself than watch poor Gary's side being massacred."

"You can't go on, Carrie," he says.
"Why not? I'll be a substitute."
Luckily I had my good strong
lace-up shoes on, because that field
was turning into a sea of mud.

"Just keep an eye on little Gavin,"
I said. "Put his dummy back in if it
drops out."

Then I was on the field. They all
looked a bit surprised.

"Come on, Skimpole Street," I called.

My dad taught me years ago to play football. In the end I was better than the boys. Even they had to admit it. And I still enjoy an occasional kickabout with my Gary.

I got the ball off the tall, skinny boy in no time at all. He just stood there with his mouth open while I tackled him. Then I went up the field with the ball at my toe, and Skimpole Street behind me. It was a wonderful feeling. I could hear the referee blowing his stupid whistle behind me somewhere.

"I'm Gibson's substitute!" I shouted over my shoulder, and kept going. The defence hadn't a chance. I sold them a dummy as easy as anything, then as the keeper started to go for his right, I gave the ball a left-footer which sent it neatly into the back of the net. The Skimpole Streeters raised a cheer. There's nothing like scoring a goal to make you feel really satisfied.

"Well done, Mum," said Gary.

"One down, eighteen to go," I said. "We'll beat them yet."

Then up came the referee.

"What do you think you're doing? This is a schools football match."

"Yes, well, I'm the Skimpole Street substitute."

"Are you a pupil?" he asks, with a

nasty sneer on his face.

"I'm on the PTA Committee. If that's not official, I don't know what is. Now, shall we kick off again?"

"Madam," says the ref, taking a deep breath, "I must ask you to leave the field. According to the rules of football, substitutes may only join the game by prior arrangement with the referee, and only while play is stopped. Improper substitutes are not permitted."

"Improper? Are you calling me improper?"

He stood there with his arms folded. He looked just like my little Gavin does if you take a jam doughnut away from him.

"Madam, either you leave the field, or I will abandon the game without more ado."

I could see he meant it. I didn't know then that a dog had just bitten his bottom, but I could see he was in a funny state of mind. His eyes had a wobbly look.

"I've been a referee for twenty years," he said, "and I've never had a day like this."

"Very well," I said, keeping my dignity. "The referee's decision is final. I know the rules. Is it fair? No. Is it just? No. But keep your hair on. I can

tell when I'm not wanted. I will
withdraw. But at least you could allow
the goal."

"Certainly not."

"What a rotter," I muttered, as I
went back to the sidelines. But the
Skimpole Streeters gave me a cheer,
and I waved back to them. I didn't
stay, though. It was too painful to
watch.

Now they've elected me to be their
Chief Trainer, and we have sessions
every Wednesday. If I don't turn them
into the best school side in the land,
my name's not Carrie Sandford. And
I've started the Skimpole Street PTA
Ladies' Team. We've already issued a
challenge to the Stapleton Road mums.
We'll make mincemeat of them!
Actually, in view of what happened at
half-time in the boys' match, that's a

rather tasteless way to put it. Let's just say we'll trounce them.

6. The Centre-Half
(Gary Sandford)

MY DAD'S A SAILOR. He's on a nuclear submarine. I can't tell you any more, because it's top secret. Except I can say this, he's the most important man on the ship. He's not the captain, he's the cook.

"After three months under water, the only thing that keeps them sane is my Chicken Rissoles," he says. When he went off last time, he said to me:

"Gary, you're the man of the house now. Take care of your mum for me, won't you. You know what a helpless little thing she is."

64

Then he winked at me and jumped into the minicab with his holdall quick before my mum could get at him.

"Gary Sandford can't even take care of his own socks," she shouted, but he was already away.

"Right," said my mum. "If you're looking after me, you can start by making me a nice cup of tea."

"You've just had one, with Dad," I said.

"Well, I want another one."

She's always a bit sniffly after my dad goes off on one of his tours of duty. I went into the kitchen with Gavin to put the kettle on again, and I heard her talking to herself in the sitting-room.

"Pull yourself together, Carrie Sandford," she was saying. "Don't be a snibbling driveller."

That's one of our jokes. Any time little Gavin cries, she says to him: "Don't be a dribbling sniveller. Or do I mean a snivelling dribbler? Or a snibbling driveller?"

What's all this got to do with that

terrible football match? Well, my mum
never drank the tea I made. She came
bursting through into the kitchen and
said:

"Come on, you landlubbers, outside!
We'll have a kickabout, to take our
mind off things."

No one else's mum plays football with them. My mum doesn't care what anyone thinks, though. She spends hours taking penalty kicks or trying out different tackles. So I wasn't really surprised to see her coming on to the field.

There were only two good things about that match. One was my mum coming on and scoring a goal. I know she wasn't supposed to, but she was terrific. The whole side cheered her when she went off.

The other good thing was the ride in the ambulance. I've always wanted to be in an ambulance that goes racing along with its blue lights flashing and its siren going wee-ooo, wee-ooo, wee-ooo, and all the traffic pulling out of its way to let it through. The only trouble was that I was feeling too bad

to really appreciate it, even when we went screaming through a red traffic light. Everything else was terrible. I don't even want to think about it.

7. The Second Defender (Norman Brown)

I DON'T KNOW what Kevin said, but whatever it was, don't believe it. He's a rotten little liar.

Of course, I was just trying to help him out a bit. He's not as fast as me, because he's too lazy to train properly, so I thought I should cover a bit more of the ground. Also, not that I'm boasting, I've got more talent than he has.

Was he grateful? He's never grateful. Instead of saying thank you, he hits me. Well, I wasn't going to take that from him. I'll tell you something about

Kevin. He still sleeps with his thumb
in his mouth. He's a bit of a baby,
really. He always waits to see what I
do, then he does it too, or wants to.

He's jealous, of course, just because
I'm the older twin. Our mum says she
wishes she'd never told us who came
first. But I can't help being first, can I?
That entitles me to say he's my little
brother, doesn't it?

I knew Kevin was in a bad mood,
that day. He was moaning about his
sore ear. He's always got an ache or a
pain somewhere. He's not a healthy
type like me. Then he complained at
breakfast because I took three
Weetabix and only left two for him.
Well, I was there first. He would have
done the same to me.

He'd been in a sulk ever since,
pretending to be still hungry, even

though he had four big slices of toast
and peanut butter. I saw him looking
into his peanut butter jar and making
a face. Anyone else wouldn't notice
that some of it had gone, but greedy
old Kevin notices everything to do
with food.

Luckily, he doesn't know it was me
that took some. I only borrowed a little
bit. Well, a fairly little bit. I say I like

the crunchy sort better, but I don't really. But Kevin said he liked smooth peanut butter, and if I'd said, "I do too," he'd say, "Copy cat, copy cat, go and eat a mouldy rat." Anyway, I don't want to like the same sort of peanut butter as Kevin.

I don't like to put the blame on others, but it was all Kevin's fault the samosas got spilled. When Mr Watkins told us to pick up the trays, I knew he was going to do something. He was going to give me a kick or a shove, I could just tell. So I gave him a push, sort of, quite a gentle one. Just to let him know not to try anything clever. But he's so clumsy. His tray tipped over, then he fell against me and made me drop my tray, and all the samosas went in a heap. Then he had the nerve to say it was my fault! I would have

given him a good thumping, if
Windbag Watkins wasn't standing
right over us.

That's something else about Kevin. He always has to put the blame on someone else. It's never his fault. Oh, no, good little Kevin never does anything wrong. And he gets away with everything. It had to be me that ate one of the wrong samosas, not him. And then he said it served me right! I'm going to put worms in his bed.

IN MY VIEW, Skimpole Street did jolly

8. The Headmaster
(Mr Gareth Watkins)

IN MY VIEW, Skimpole Street did jolly
well, jolly well. Yes, we lost. Yes, we
were disqualified from the competition.
Yes, the game had to be abandoned
after the unpleasant scenes at
half-time. Yes, the police interviewed
Mr Abdullah of the Genghis Khan
Fast Food Takeaway. But in the end
nothing could be definitely proved, and
there were no charges. And young
Patel and his team tried really hard.
Most of them did, anyway.

However big the disaster, always
Think Positive, that's what I always do

myself, and that's the advice I give my pupils, too. Look at the plus side. We have our fine new football kit for when we're allowed to rejoin the inter-schools football league. And the lads have learned a lot from their defeat. With Mrs Sandford now as Chief Trainer, they are becoming a really strong side. Young Bayram Abdullah has got very keen on football, and is beginning to look, well, if not exactly slim, certainly less stout than before.

I know that Mr Abdullah meant well. It was kind of him to offer to supply half-time refreshments. When I was a boy in the Welsh Valleys we were lucky to get half an orange to suck at half-time.

"This is a feast, a perfect feast, Mr Abdullah," I said, when he arrived

with his little van and started to
unload trays of food. In fact, I had to
ask him to leave most of it aside, for
after the match. It's not good to eat too
much right in the middle of the game.
But Mr Abdullah was particularly
keen that they should at least sample
the samosas.

"I've prepared two lots, Mr
Watkins. One for Skimpole Street,
that's this tray here, and that one for
the enemy."

"The enemy, Mr Abdullah? It's only
a game, you know."

"I was watching that first half, Mr
Watkins," he said. "Until I had to go
and collect the food. They were
murdering our poor boys. But we'll see
what happens in the second half."

He had a curious gleam in his eye,

but I thought nothing of it at the time.

Mr Abdullah went to fetch some drinks from his van, and I saw the Brown twins standing about idly. That's something I can't abide.

"Come on, you two. Do something useful. Kevin, take this tray to the Stapleton Road side. Norman, pass this one around our own lot. Carefully, now."

Did Norman bump Kevin, or did Kevin bump Norman? It's always hard to tell with the Brown twins. Anyway, no sooner had these two boys picked up their trays than they seemed to collide, and the samosas all fell in a heap on the floor. Kevin glared at Norman. Norman glared at Kevin.

"You pushed me."

"Please sir, he pushed me."

"Never mind, never mind, pick them up. Quickly, now. Wretched boys."

Luckily it was a clean part of the floor, and the pastries looked none the worse for their little accident. Kevin stomped off to the Stapleton Road side with his tray. I sampled one of the samosas myself. It was deliciously warm and spicy.

"Jolly good," I said to Mr Abdullah, who had come back in with a carton of rather unsuitable fizzy drink cans.

"You've done us proud, Mr Abdullah, proud, what with the new strip and these excellent refreshments as well."

"It was nothing," said Mr Abdullah, politely. "Did the enem– the other team get their samosas?"

"Indeed they did," I told him. "The two lots got a bit mixed up, as it happens, but of course that doesn't matter a bit."

"Oh, no!" cried Mr Abdullah, looking suddenly horrified. He turned to the boys.

"Don't eat them! Don't touch those samosas."

Even as he spoke, young Vernon
Cramb uttered a wail, clutched his
stomach, and dashed out of the room.
The tray of samosas was almost empty.
Eleven hungry boys don't take long to
clear the decks.

Gary Sandford gave a low moan and
followed Cramb out of the room at
high speed. Mr Abdullah turned to
me, his eyes filled with dismay.

"This has all gone terribly wrong!"
he cried.

"What do you mean?"

"They should not have been mixed up. Our boys should not have eaten the other team's samosas."

"But why ever not?"

"I put a little something into them, Mr Watkins. Quite harmless, really. Just to give our boys a chance, you see . . ."

Unfortunately, I could not wait to hear the rest of his explanation.

Something very strange was happening inside me. It was as if several angry hedgehogs had started fighting in my stomach. I had to make a run for the door, pushing past Mr Davis, the referee, who was looking green and shouting something about being poisoned.

Willoughby Park's pavilion does not boast a telephone, but old Mr Hitchin

saw it was an emergency, whizzed off in his wheelchair, and rang for an ambulance.

Needless to say, the game was abandoned. Apart from myself and the referee, five of our side and six from Stapleton Road were affected by the doctored samosas. The effect very soon wore off, and they didn't keep us in hospital. Once they'd pumped our stomachs out, they said we could go home.

But Mr Davis the referee was bitter, very bitter.

"I shall be making a full report of everything," he said to me. "If I do nothing else before I give up being a referee for ever, I shall make sure that your school is banned from the inter-school league for a very long time."

"Come now, Mr Davis," I said. "Let's Think Positive about this. I'm sure there are extenuating circumstances."

"Extenuating poppycock!" he snapped. "I have been kicked by a boy, attacked by a dog, insulted by a woman, and finally poisoned. Perhaps you'd like to set my hair on fire, or hit me on the head with a hammer, just to round things off."

"Now, now. You're not yourself. You'll feel better tomorrow, I'm sure."

"If I survive until then," he said, coldly. "Goodbye. You will hear from my solicitors."

Some people just can't see the Positive Side, can they?

Now I always say that no experience is so bad that you can't draw something positive from it. And it

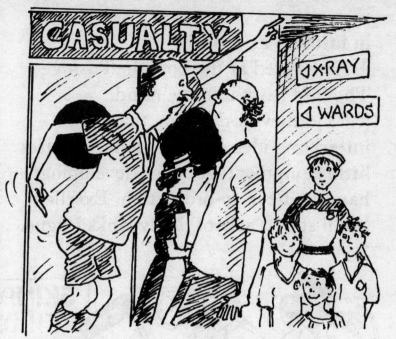

happened again this time. It was actually young Ashton Jackson who gave me the idea. Fortunately he had eaten nothing at half-time, or I would never have heard the end of it from Mrs Jackson.

"What have you learned from the match, Ashton?" I asked the lad.

"I think I'll stick to tiddlywinks

in future," he replied.

As I gazed at the boy, the Positive Thought leapt into my mind.

"Tiddlywinks? Hmm, that's an interesting idea. Indoor game, requires little equipment, good for developing hand-and-eye co-ordination. Excellent. We'll start a school tiddlywinks league.

Who knows, it may become a craze and sweep the country. And it will all have started at Skimpole Street School. We'll have television crews round, newspapers . . . "

I thought I heard young Jackson murmur, "Oh, no." But I may have been mistaken.

9. The Inside Right (Bayram Abdullah)

FOOTBALL IS TOPS! I love it. I always wanted to play, but they always said I was too fat. I only got picked for the game with Stapleton Road because my dad donated the strip. Patel told me.

"Just try and keep out of the way," he said. "If the ball comes to you, kick it to one of us. If you can."

But I was the one who nearly created a goal for us. And he missed the penalty kick. He scored a beaut on someone's greenhouse, though. I thought the match was great. Even though it was only half a game, and it rained nearly all the time, and we were beaten twenty-two nothing, and got covered in mud, it was still good fun. It's nice to be part of a team. And next time, I want to take the penalty.

I won't miss.

DAVID ROSS

How we got back into

the Inter-Schools
Football Competition

Illustrated by
Jacqui Thomas

Chapter 1

WHEN BILLY GRAY came to Skimpole Street School, he was very quiet for a whole week. Then one day, in the middle of Quiet Reading, he let out a loud squeal. Everybody looked up.

"Whatever is the matter, Billy?" asked the teacher, Miss Goodwin.

"Nothing, miss," he mumbled, with his hand to his ear. "I got earache, suddenly."

"Well, you gave us all a fright. Tell me if it gets too bad again, don't wait until you have to scream."

The pain was not inside Billy's ear

but on the outside, where a paper pellet had hit it. He knew who had done it. It was Norman Brown, sitting a few desks away. Norman was grinning proudly, holding up his ruler and bending it backwards in a way that was supposed to let everyone see except the teacher.

"Are you getting on with your reading, Norman?" she asked.

"Yes, miss," said Norman, turning in a hurry to his book.

At break Norman came up to Billy. Norman's twin brother, Kevin, was with him, and so was a boy called Jason Cooper. Everyone called Jason "Piano Legs" because he – well, thought Billy, it's a name that suits him, no doubt about that. They looked at Billy and he looked at them.

"Well, he didn't tell," said Norman.

Billy Gray looked over at the wall and whistled quietly through his teeth.

"Well, ask him, then," said Kevin.

"I'm going to ask him," said Norman. "Don't push me, kid. Give me space."

"Huh, you can have all the space you like as far as I'm concerned," said his brother.

"OK," said Norman. He fixed Billy with his pale, slightly piggy eyes. "Do you want to play football?"

Norman hadn't said thanks, and he hadn't said sorry. Billy Gray somehow thought that he wasn't very likely to do either of these things. Maybe inviting him to play football was Norman's way of doing it.

"I'm not really into football," he said. "But, OK."

"I'm not really into football," said Kevin, jerking his head from side to side and mimicking Billy's voice.

"Come on then," said Norman.

Other boys came running to join them. Billy had got to know most of their names. There was Gary Sandford, a solid-looking, grinning boy with very short hair. There was Sarvindar Patel, bright-eyed, black-haired. Billy Gray stood on the football ground as the others ran to take up positions.

"He's in your team," Norman Brown shouted to Piano Legs. There were only six in each side.

"My kick-off," said Norman, and without waiting, he gave the ball a little nudge with his foot, and followed it in little zigzags down the pitch.

"Tackle him, somebody," roared Piano Legs Cooper from the goalmouth, which was marked out by two jackets on the ground. Someone ran at Norman, but Norman got past him and came on, until his twin, Kevin, swerved in front of him, took the ball away and passed it back up the field. Everyone ran after it, except Billy. There was a clumsy tackle at the goalmouth, a corner, and then the ball came flying back down. Piano Legs

rushed out and scooped it up in his arms, held it for a moment, then tossed it to Billy, who had not yet moved.

"Are you in the game or aren't you?" he yelled.

Billy Gray held the ball against his foot. For a moment everything seemed still. Then he saw Norman come thundering towards him. Better do

something, he thought, and tapped the ball gently forwards, running with it at his toe. Transferring it from left to right, he dodged past Norman with ease, hearing a gasp of surprise behind him. He went on up the field, passing in between the opposition players as if they had been as still as traffic cones, and from ten metres punted it gently between the goalpost jackets, in exactly the opposite side the goalie expected. A cheer went up from Piano Legs at the far end. But most of the others were too amazed to say anything.

"I thought you said you couldn't play," said Kevin, hoarsely.

"I didn't say I couldn't. I said I wasn't really into it."

Kevin just gazed at him, open-mouthed. The thought of someone who could play football like that, not wanting to play, was too much for him.

"You must practise, though," said Gary Sandford.

"Not really."

Gary was silent. He practised all the time, but he knew he could never get the ball to behave like that for him. "Wait till my mum hears about this," he said.

"Your mum?" It was Billy's turn to be surprised.

"Yeah, she's our trainer. For the school team. You've got to be in it. Now we'll really have a chance of getting back into the league."

Chapter 2

"I JUST DON'T believe it."

Mrs Carrie Sandford, mother of Gary, put her teacup down on the saucer with a clatter.

"That boy is a natural," she said. "I've never seen anything like it. He can make the ball do anything he wants. It's uncanny. With him in the side, and the way I've trained up the others, Skimpole Street could be the best school team in the country. But he doesn't want to know." Her voice rose. "He – won't – join – the – team."

She was sitting in the headmaster's

office a few days later. Never had Mr Watkins seen her in such a state. He put on a soothing expression.

"Well now, Mrs Sandford, I agree with you, I agree. But we can't make

him join the football team. It's not in the National Curriculum, you know."

It was break-time, and Mrs Sandford looked out of the window.

"There he is, playing now," she said bitterly, "when it doesn't matter. But that's not the worst of it. You know why he won't join the team? He hasn't got the time. He goes to ballet class. He wants to be a dancer!"

On Mrs Sandford's lips, the word "dancer" sounded like "shoplifter" or "cat-torturer". Mr Watkins's frown grew deeper.

"Now, Mrs Sandford, I must differ from you there. There's nothing wrong with dancing, nothing at all. It's —"

"You can think what you like," said Carrie Sandford, forgetting her manners in the heat of her feeling. "What sort of boy would want to go to ballet classes rather than play in the school football team? If one of my boys did that, I'd soon make him see sense."

She brightened up a little. "Maybe I could talk to his mother?"

"Oh, I don't think that would do much good, Mrs Sandford. The thing is, I don't know if you know, but Billy's mother actually gives the dancing classes."

"I see," said Mrs Sandford. "This may be more difficult than I thought. But still, wouldn't it be wonderful for Skimpole Street to be top of the Inter-Schools League? I'm sure they'll re-admit us to the competition next year. All we have to do is show them what we can do in matches like that friendly against Winterton Juniors next week. The committee'll soon have forgotten all about that, that . . ."

"Please don't remind me about that awful day, Mrs Sandford," said the headmaster, shuddering. He would never forget the time when Skimpole Street had been beaten 22–nil, and thrown out of the league.

Mrs Sandford sighed.

"Well, I must be going. Thanks for the tea, Mr Watkins. Keep hoping. Bye, now."

But Skimpole Street School's first and only eleven had to play without the help of Billy Gray. When Carrie arrived after school for a training session, she gazed bitterly at Billy as he set off for dancing class with his bag slung over his back.

"It just isn't fair," she murmured.

Chapter 3

GARY SANDFORD HAD never thought he would be friendly with a boy who went to dancing class.

"What do you do there?" he asked Billy one day at school.

"Lots of different exercises," said Billy. "We have to warm up first, otherwise you're likely to pull a muscle . . . Why don't you come and watch one day? My mum wouldn't mind."

"Do you really not like football? I don't understand how you got to be so good if you don't play?" asked Gary.

"Well, I did play and I do like it, but

113

I like dancing too and my mum said there wasn't time for both, so I had to choose which to do . . ." Billy shrugged.

Billy kept his dancing kit in a blue cotton bag with B.G. embroidered in red and a skull and crossbones in white on it. He took it to school with him on Mondays and Thursdays, which were his dancing days. They also happened to be the football training days.

That afternoon, as everyone was streaming out at the end of school, Billy went to his hook to find his dancing bag, and it wasn't there. For a moment he stared at the empty space, wondering if it was the wrong hook. Then he looked around. The only people about were a few of the boys who did football training.

"Hey, has anyone seen my blue bag?" he called.

They looked round.

"No," they said, innocently.

"Maybe you forgot to bring it," said Piano Legs.

"No, I remember hanging it up."

They went off, leaving Billy standing helplessly. Only Gary remained.

"Someone's taken it," said Billy.

Gary frowned. There didn't seem to be any other answer.

"I haven't much time," said Billy, worriedly. "My mum gets really cross if people turn up late."

"What's in it?" asked Gary.

"All the stuff I need – shoes, tights . . ."

"Come on, Gary!" a voice shouted from outside.

"You go," said Billy. "I'll just have to explain." He didn't look as if he was looking forward to it.

*

Goalposts had already been marked out in the usual way, with coats, and, as Gary came on to the field, he saw a little corner of blue sticking out from under a folded-up green coat.

"Get a move on, Gary Sandford," shouted his mother. "You're slower than a one-legged tortoise."

But he went to take a closer look at the blue corner, bent down, and pulled out a blue bag with a white skull and crossbones on it.

"Who put that there?" he said.

Nobody answered, but he saw a huge, broad, pleased grin spreading helplessly across Norman Brown's face.

"I'll be back!" he shouted, and raced off with the bag towards the playground gate, ignoring the shouts from behind.

He could see Billy in the street far

ahead and, with pounding feet, he ran
to catch him up, and thrust the bag at
him as the other boy turned in surprise.

"Found it," he gasped. "Must get
back. See you in the morning."

Gary Sandford's father had been a
cook in the Navy, until the Navy

discovered it didn't need so many cooks, and now he was looking for another job. Meanwhile, he cooked for his family, and that evening they were eating his pork rissoles with spinach and creamed potatoes.

"It was Norman Brown, I suppose," said Mrs Sandford. "Well, it wasn't

right to take Billy's bag and hide it, whoever it was. And I suppose it just had to be my Gary who found it and gave it back."

She gave Gary a long, inspecting look. He knew what it was for. She was looking for any signs that he was about to turn into a ballet dancer.

"You're hopeless," said Kevin Brown to Norman Brown, in the privacy of their bedroom. "You idiot. Why did you leave that bit of his bag sticking out? You can't even hide a little bag properly. If we can't stop Billy going to dancing classes, he'll never join the football team, and we'll never get back into the league. Why did I get you for a brother?"

"Well, I certainly didn't ask for you," growled Norman. "And I was born

120

first, so you couldn't have asked for me anyway. Just remember, you're the little one. So pipe down, Baby Kevin."

"And then you let Gary Sandford walk off with it."

"Well, what was I supposed to do – take it off him, right in front of his mother?"

"You couldn't have got it off him anyway."

"Oh yes I could."

"Oh no you couldn't. Remember that time when he –"

But Norman never wanted to remember any time when anyone else had got the better of him, and quickly changed the subject.

"Hey, I've got an idea," he cried. "Let's follow Billy along to his dancing class and then stick up a sign in the window saying 'FOOTBALL RULES' and run off before anyone sees us. Shall we?"

"Yeah. Great idea, I love it," said Kevin enthusiastically.

The Brown twins were friends again.

Chapter 4

THERE WERE ABOUT fifteen minutes to full time. The score was 2–1, with Skimpole Street in the lead against Winterton Junior School, and hanging on by the tips of their fingernails against determined attacking play from the other side. It was a cold, dry day with the wind blowing across the pitch, making it hard to control the ball. As they watched, it was kicked high from the Winterton half and came down towards Charlie Gibson. He rose elegantly to take the header, and sent it back upfield, but a wayward gust blew

the ball over to the side where a
Winterton player just happened to be
waiting. He grabbed his chance and
sent a low pass towards the ten-yard

line, where one of his own forwards was racing to meet it. Not a Skimpole Street player in sight. Only Piano Legs Cooper, crouched at the corner of his goal, waiting to catch it.

It was a perfect shot. With one smooth stroke the Winterton forward sent the ball flying onwards and upwards. Piano Legs leapt for it like a hero, but the ball slipped just above his outstretched hands and fell into the back of the net. A cheer went up. The little group of Skimpole Street supporters exchanged worried glances.

"Ten minutes," said Mr Watkins.

"They're too tired," said Carrie. "They can't run any more. They just aren't fit enough."

"They're running their hearts out," said the headmaster. "Win, draw or lose, I'm proud of them. Proud."

"I want a win," said Mrs Sandford. "Or they'll get a piece of my mind, afterwards. They've run out of puff too soon. Too many videos and cream doughnuts and not enough exercise, that's the trouble, if you ask me." She turned away, to shout at the team: "Come on, Skimpole Street, get moving. We need a goal!"

But suddenly, it seemed as if Winterton were swarming all over the Skimpole Street end. Looking up wearily, Gary Sandford felt as if there were twenty-two rather than eleven of them. He could scarcely see a Skimpole player. A group of Winterton players seemed to be taking the ball down-field all by themselves. Then he saw a green-and-yellow-clad shape on the move. It was the solid figure of Skimpole Street's inside-right, Bayram Abdullah. Bayram

126

at full charge was quite something, and he cut through between two of the other side and took the ball, rather like a tank between two bicycles.

"Gary!" shouted Sarvindar Patel, running to take position by the far corner, and pointing to midfield.

Seeing Sarvindar go, Gary felt some energy return to his tired legs, and he ran to keep up with Bayram. Now the field was almost clear but for the three of them and the Winterton goalie, his arms outspread. Bayram passed the ball over to Gary, who took it on the inside of his foot, remembering how Billy Gray did it, but he could never manage that effortless transfer from foot to foot. He was just about to pass the ball to the waving figure of Sarvindar, when something heavy knocked into him and sent him to the ground. The whistle blew shrilly. It was a Winterton defender, rushing back, too keen or too rough. Bruised and dizzy, Gary got to his feet. A free kick.

"Do you want to take it?" Sarvindar was asking, but Gary shook his head. He couldn't even see straight just then, never mind take a kick. Bayram moved forward instead. A few quick steps were enough to get all his weight behind the ball. The keeper never had a chance. The ball roared past him into the back of the net. Bayram Abdullah's face had a smile of perfect happiness. It was his very first goal in a proper match. Five minutes later the whistle went. Skimpole Street had won.

Skimpole Street played more friendlies. But they did not win any more. The players were getting tired and fed up

with losing. Mrs Sandford was tired too.
On one training evening, only five of
the side turned up. Carrie sent them
home again.

"What is the matter with these boys?"
she asked, when she got home.

"Don't push them too hard, Carrie,"
said her husband. "It's only a game,
you know."

"Huh!" she said. "That's just where you're wrong. It's not a game. It's Them or Us. I just want to make sure it's Us that end up on top. The next game is a real clincher. An inspector from the Inter-Schools League is coming to watch us. And guess who we'll be playing? Stapleton Road."

"What? The ones who –?"

"That's right. The ones who beat us 22–nil. It's taken a long time to arrange this game, and if anything goes wrong this time, we're out in the cold for ever."

Chapter 5

GARY SANDFORD, FEELING rather shy, sat on a bench at the side of the Mossop Memorial Hall, and watched Billy's dancing class. There were ten girls in leotards, and one boy in a white T-shirt and black tights. A lady sat at a black piano at one side of the hall, and Billy's mother stood in the centre of the floor. Mrs Gray was small, hardly taller than Billy, with dark hair pulled back and tied in a bun. She had smiled at Gary.

"You're welcome to watch," she said.

"It's nice for Billy to have a friend who takes an interest in dance."

"Ooh, Gary Sandford," squeaked Margery O'Neill. "Are you going to join the class?"

"No fear," he muttered, beginning to wish he hadn't come. Then Mrs Gray clapped her hands, and the class began.

*

Winking at each other, trying not to giggle with excitement, the Brown twins parked their bikes by the gate. Kevin had a large piece of cardboard tucked under his arm. Taking huge, tiptoeing steps, they approached the back of the hall.

"What a surprise they'll get," chortled Kevin.

"Let's take a look in through the window first," whispered Norman. "You can give me a leg up."

"Why me? Why don't you give me a leg up?" hissed Kevin. "Why is it always –"

"Sssh, they'll hear us."

Faintly from inside they could hear the notes of the piano.

"You can have a go after me," said Norman. "It was my idea so I should be first. Then we'll stick the sign up."

Kevin went down on all fours and Norman stood on his back, got his arms over the window sill, and struggled to hoist himself higher.

"Oof! Aagh!" grunted Kevin when his brother slipped and two large feet suddenly landed on his back. Norman was no lightweight. But, at last, standing on the protesting Kevin's shoulders, Norman was able to get his head above the sill, and look through into the hall.

Gary Sandford, sitting at the side, was the only one who noticed when, like a rising moon, Norman Brown's big round face suddenly appeared against the glass. The sight of Norman roused Gary to action. He rose from his bench and slipped quietly along to the door at the far end, marked EMERGENCY EXIT. Pushing it open, he ran out, ready to do battle.

But as he ran, his foot struck against a brick lying hidden in the grass, and he overbalanced, twisting his leg and feeling a sickening, cracking wrench in his ankle as he did so. He gave a shout of agony and lay still. Mrs Gray appeared at the door, to see him lying there. Norman and Kevin were receding rapidly down the road, pedalling madly, as if they were being chased by an angry tiger. Lying on the ground by Gary was a tatty sign saying 'FOOTBALL ROOLS!'

Chapter 6

"IT'S A HOODOO," said Mrs Sandford gloomily. "We'll never get back into the Inter-Schools League. First, Gary breaks his ankle. And now I've been told I need to do evening practice drives round all the bus routes before I sit my PSV test. That means I won't be able to take the training sessions. And even that's not all. Guess what day they've set my test for? You've got it – the Stapleton Road game. It's just not fair. What can we do?"

"I've got an idea," said Billy Gray, who had come to have tea with Gary.

"If she would do it. The training times would have to be changed, though."

"Who? What? You aren't making sense," said Mrs Sandford.

"My mum," said Billy. "She might take over the training, if I asked her."

"But does your mum know anything about football?" From the sound of her voice, Mrs Sandford was not very keen on anyone else's mum taking over her team.

"Not much, but I do. And she knows lots about teaching people how to move – not just in dancing. She could do that, and I could help with the football bits, maybe . . ." His voice trailed away. It seemed silly and he wished he hadn't said it. But Gary's mum was sitting with her hands on her knees, staring at him, her mouth slightly open.

"But then, you'd be in the team," she said.

"Yeah, I suppose so," he mumbled, looking down at his plate. "If I was picked."

Suddenly he felt a smack between the shoulder-blades that almost pressed his face into the mound of mashed potato on his plate. Mrs Sandford had jumped to her feet and delivered the monster pat on the back.

"Fan-tastic," she said. Suddenly she was as cheerful as a squirrel who has found a whole bag of nuts. "You're picked."

"But I don't know if my mum will do it," Billy said, beginning to worry.

"I'll talk to her," said Mrs Sandford. "Just eat up. You're going to need all the energy you've got."

*

"You're so clever, aren't you?" said Kevin Brown to his twin brother. They were sitting gloomily in their bedroom. Their TV set had been taken away for a week, as a punishment, and they did not know what to do. So they argued.

"Shut up," said Norman.

"You and your stupid ideas."

"You came along too."

"Well, whose idea was it to look in through the window?"

"Anyway," said Norman angrily, "I got all bruised when I fell off that window sill, and nobody cares. Gary Sandford trips by accident and breaks his ankle and everyone's sorry for him. But what about me? I can hardly move. Ouch," he added, in a pained tone, in case Kevin had not got the point.

"You ran fast enough to get to your bike," said Kevin.

"Not as fast as you," said Norman. "Brave-hero Kevin was halfway down the road already."

"Anyway, now see what's happened all because of you – we're both barred from the football team by Windbag Watkins. Not just you – me too."

"I don't care," said Norman. "I'll show them they can't treat me like that.

Old Windbag forgot about one thing."

"What's that?"

Norman's grin returned. "Never mind. I'm not telling you," he said, smugly. "You can just wait and see."

"No, no, Mr Gregory, I'm sure everything will be fine. Perfectly fine. You'll have absolutely nothing to worry

about." Mr Gareth Watkins was speaking on the telephone to the headmaster of Stapleton Road School, who was also the Secretary of the Inter-Schools League, to confirm the arrangements for the friendly match. Once again they were to play at Willoughby Park, scene of the epic defeat.

Despite his soothing voice, Mr Watkins did not feel confident when he put down the receiver. He had an uneasy, hollow feeling in the pit of his stomach, as if a disaster was about to happen. It was all getting very like the last time they had played Stapleton Road. Skimpole Street had lost one of its best players in young Sandford. He himself had sacked the Brown twins from the team. They were not specially good players, but there were no better

ones to replace them. The trainer, Mrs Sandford, who had done such a good job up to now, was suddenly too busy with her bus-driving lessons. And now the football team was being trained by a ballet teacher! He groaned faintly. No doubt young Gray's mother meant well. But ballet and football – they were two different worlds!

Chapter 7

"DID YOU SAY skipping?"

"Yeah."

"You're doing skipping? With a skipping rope? Like girls do?"

"Yeah, that's right. And other stuff too. Breathing."

"Everybody breathes, stupid."

"But it's how you breathe that makes a difference."

"I don't believe it."

Norman Brown and Bayram Abdullah were talking in the playground. Norman couldn't help hanging around during the training sessions.

"I don't believe it," repeated Norman, tittering. "You wouldn't catch me skipping if I was in the team."

"Well, you're not, are you?" pointed out Bayram, and trotted off to the training session, leaving Norman with nothing to do but to go home and pick a fight with Kevin.

At the training ground, Gary Sandford's mum was in her Skimpole Street PTA Ladies' Football Team tracksuit, with a whistle on a cord round her neck. Billy Gray's mum was beside her.

"I'm so grateful to you for helping out," said Carrie Sandford.

"It's a pleasure," said Mrs Gray.

"They look fitter already," said Carrie. "I see now that I've been so busy teaching them basic footballing skills that I've neglected things like physical fitness. But I really don't know anything about all that. With you teaching them how to keep fit, and me teaching them the tricks of the game, we'll make them winners yet."

She took the whistle and handed it to Mrs Gray.

"Oh, I don't need that," said Mrs Gray, handing it back.

She clapped her hands quite quietly, and suddenly all the boys, who had been dashing about, came and stood in a row in front of her, ready for action.

"Well, knock me down," said Carrie in amazement. "I have to blow my

whistle three times and shout my head off before they pay any attention. It's a miracle."

Chapter 8

THE MATCH WITH Stapleton Road
School was to be played at Willoughby
Park.

The team from Stapleton Road
arrived in a minibus, with their
headmaster, Mr Gregory, their PT
teacher, and the referee, Mr Archer.
Sarvindar Patel looked over his team
as they laced their boots. Piano Legs
was there, and Charlie Gibson, and
Bayram Abdullah. Billy Gray was
there too, in the Skimpole Street green
shirt and yellow shorts for the first
time. The sight of all these gave him

some encouragement. Then he looked at the others. Vincent O'Neill, Terry Bartlett, Simon Hawke, Lee Stoker, Tony Smith and Jasper Jensen. He had even persuaded Ashton Jackson to come along as reserve. Ashton was an ace player – at tiddlywinks. He had once said he would never play football again, and he had only agreed to come so long as he was not expected to actually touch the ball, or tackle, or run. Though he grinned cheerfully at them, Sarvindar felt his confidence melt away. He missed the reliable face of Gary Sandford. He even missed Norman and Kevin Brown. Say what you like, thought Sarvindar, they were strong players, always ready to tackle.

More than half his team had done very little training, and what training they had done was of a rather strange sort. Behind his bright smile, Sarvindar was dreading this match.

"Are we ready then, boys?" asked Mr Watkins. "Have we the ball? Who's the ball monitor? Oh, my goodness!" His mouth dropped open in consternation. "How could I have forgotten. Norman Brown was ball monitor. Is he here?"

"No, Mr Watkins," chorused the team.

"Are we all set then, Mr Watkins?" boomed a voice. It was Mr Gregory, from Stapleton Road School.

"Just a . . . just a small technical hitch, Mr Gregory," said Mr Watkins. "We don't seem to actually have a ball."

"No ball, Mr Watkins?" Mr Gregory did not look surprised. He looked as if he had expected nothing else.

"I'm sure there's a simple explanation," said Mr Watkins, looking around desperately.

"Please, sir," said Billy Gray, "Gary Sandford has a proper football. I could ride over to his house and get it, and bring it back."

"Good thinking, yes, do that," said Mr Watkins. "Be as quick as you can, not forgetting road safety, of course, mind you."

But when Billy reached Gary's house and rang the doorbell, there was no answer. Then he remembered. Gary's dad was first taking his mum to the bus

depot for her driving test, and then taking Gary on to the football match.

He turned away, and was just about to get on his bike again, when he saw Norman Brown approaching along the street.

"Hey, Norman," he said. "We were looking for you at Willoughby Park. You're the ball monitor."

"Why should I have to be the ball monitor when I'm not allowed in the team? Old Windbag can do it himself."

"But where is it? We must have a ball to play the match."

Norman shrugged his shoulders and did not answer, but he couldn't stop his grin, which spread across his face until it seemed to reach from ear to ear.

Billy Gray wanted to knock the grin off Norman Brown's face. But he resisted the urge.

"Look, Norman," he said. "OK, you've made your point. Now give me the ball. Everyone's waiting."

"They can wait," said Norman cheerfully. Then his eyes fell on Billy's new wristwatch. He had broken his own ages ago.

"I'll tell you where the ball is if you let me wear your watch," he said.

"OK, for a week."

"A fortnight."

"Done," said Billy, unbuckling the watch.

"The ball's in our bike shed," said Norman.

"Quick, then," said Billy. "Let's go."

At Willoughby Park, things were becoming tense. Mr Watkins, Mrs Gray and the Skimpole Street team sat unhappily, waiting for Billy's return.

From behind the partition they could hear the voices of the Stapleton Road team. At one point some of them began to sing, "Why are we waiting, Oh, why are we waiting?" – until Mr Gregory's booming voice silenced them. Then the door opened and everyone looked up, hopefully. It was Mr Sandford, with his younger son,

Gavin, and Gary, whose ankle was still in plaster. But no sign of a ball.

"What's the matter?" said Mr Sandford. "I thought we'd have missed the start."

"Didn't you see young Gray?" asked Mr Watkins.

"No. We've been taking Carrie to do her test, and then came on here."

"Oh, dear." Mr Watkins sank back on to his bench. "Everything's going wrong again."

There was a knock, the door in the partition opened, and Mr Gregory's head looked through.

"Ah, Mr Watkins," he said. "One of my boys has remembered that we have an old ball under the seat in our minibus. It's not perfect, but in the circumstances we can use it. Otherwise we shall have to scrub the game and go home. We really can't sit around all day, you know."

"No, Mr Gregory, of course not. That will be fine, thank you. Come along, boys, we'll make a start."

Sarvindar Patel raised a wail.

"But, sir, Billy Gray's not back."

"We can't help it. You've got your reserve, haven't you?"

"Come on, Ashton," said Sarvindar. "You're on."

"Oh no!" Ashton Jackson looked horrified. "I've got a headache coming on. And I've had a funny feeling in my side all morning . . ."

"You'll have another sort of ache if you don't get a move on," said Sarvindar menacingly.

Chapter 9

IT WAS A fine, sunny day. The pitch was dry, the turf was newly mown, and the ball raced across it as fast and as smoothly as a hockey puck across the ice.

"Come on, Skimpole," cried Mr Watkins. Usually Mrs Sandford was beside him, screaming herself hoarse, but Mrs Gray did not call out at all.

Ten minutes into the game, and still no score. Most of the play was in the Skimpole Street half, but they were

defending strongly. And, the head-master noticed, some of them at least were showing quite a lot of skill. Bayram Abdullah no longer charged like an angry hippo. Instead, it seemed to Mr Watkins that he almost danced. He seemed to have learned how to move suddenly sideways, just one light step, taking the ball with him, leaving the other player gaping with surprise. Piano Legs was having a busy time as the backs were constantly clearing the ball back to him. But try as he might to kick it far down the field, there was no follow-up. It was clear to Mr Watkins that two or three of the Skimpole Street side were doing nearly all the work.

"They won't last out," he muttered to himself.

At that moment there was a successful rush down the left-hand side and a tall, thin Stapleton Road player blasted the ball past Piano Legs and into the net. A cheer went up from the other side of the pitch as the whistle blew. Five minutes later, there was a second goal. The Stapleton Road side had found the answer to Skimpole Street's defence.

Then Ashton suddenly gave a shout. "There he is!"

Gary looked round and saw Billy Gray cycling into the park, with a ball-shaped carrier bag clutched at the handlebars. Even from a distance, they could see his face fall as he saw that the match had already begun.

By half-time, the score was 4–nil to Stapleton Road. Mr Watkins sipped at a cup of tea and anxiously watched as Mr Gregory and the referee spoke

quietly together. At one point he saw them both shake their heads. Oh dear, he whispered, and almost made the kind of face he only made when alone in his office.

Mrs Gray was talking quietly to the team as they stood round her.

"You've done very well so far," she said. "I don't really know much about football, but I can see that you've done a wonderful job in defence. Now you have to attack. Everything's just the same. Remember your movements and timing – just enough and no more. One step at the right time is better than running all across the field. Mark each other." Her eyes were on Sarvindar Patel. "Don't try to do everything yourself. Make your team work."

Sarvindar nodded, his face serious, but inside he suddenly felt oddly cheerful, considering the score.

Ashton Jackson retired gratefully from the game at half-time. He had not touched the ball once. Billy Gray came on instead.

The captain of the Stapleton Road side took the first kick with a confident air. He saw no reason to change the formula that had brought four goals in the first half. Tipping the ball gently to the player on his left, he set out to run down the field with the other forwards. Then, to his surprise, he saw the ball

was not there. He swung round to see a Skimpole Street player halfway to the goal, the ball at his feet. A rush of green and yellow went sweeping past him as the Skimpole Street side raced into the opposition's half. He stormed up after them, shouting to his team-mates. But, before they reached the twenty-five yard line, Billy Gray had placed the ball firmly in the net.

Sarvindar Patel's heart was pounding as the goal kick was taken. The ball came bouncing over the springy turf and a Stapleton Roader ran to take possession. With two of his mates keeping pace, he was soon far down the field, and Piano Legs Cooper came out to crouch warily at the centre of the goal. Then the Stapleton player tried a long cross that rose beautifully and fell at the feet of their star player, the tall thin boy. Vincent O'Neill and Simon Hawke, in defence, looked on.

"Stop him," shouted Sarvindar. "Tackle!"

A new voice came from the sidelines. "Vincent!" shouted Mrs Gray. "Remember!"

Vincent rose on to his tiptoes, and seemed to glide across to intercept the boy with the ball. But instead of the expected direct tackle, he turned at the last moment and pushed the ball off to the right, where Simon was waiting. Simon kicked it clumsily, and the ball rose into the air, spinning, while the Stapleton players came closing in.

One of them jumped to head it at the same time as Charlie Gibson. But Charlie rose higher, springing from the ankles as he had been taught by Mrs Gray. He sent the ball on a wavering

course, but upfield again. Sarvindar saw what was happening and sent Lee and Tony upfield. The ball fell to Bayram who drove it with a powerful kick across the centre-line to where Billy, Lee and Tony were waiting. Billy took the ball, passed it quickly to Lee and, with a jerk of his head, showed him where to place it, as he himself ran

forward towards the goal. He could
hear the thudding of feet as the
Stapleton Road side, caught again by
surprise, came rushing back into
defence. Lee held the ball too long and
made a bad pass, right across the
goalmouth. It was dangerously near the
keeper, who rushed out just too late to
capture the ball. Billy had been

expecting an earlier cross and was too far back, but Tony Smith rushed on to the ball.

"Shoot!" shouted Billy.

"Shoot!" came Sarvindar's voice from somewhere behind.

Tony closed his eyes and shot. The ball flew up, just too high, hit the crossbar, and veered back on to the field. It bounced once, then Bayram Abdullah let it come to his chest and trickle down. A wall of Stapleton Road blue and white stripes seemed to face him. He brought his boots together under the ball, jumped in the air, and it rose up in front of him. In less than a second he had placed a gentle kick that sent it just over their heads and down towards Charlie Gibson. Charlie obliged with another lofty header that sent it high into the net.

By this time, the Stapleton Road side were thoroughly confused. Something had gone wrong and they did not know how to cope with it. Sarvindar Patel's eyes were shining with satisfaction.

Something was going right and he knew exactly what to do. The hours of practise on the wooden floor of the Mossop Memorial Hall now showed their value. The Stapleton Roaders ran furiously, they tackled desperately. The Skimpole Street players seemed to spend much of the time standing still, and when they moved, they did not run

in the usual way. Sometimes they took tiny steps, sometimes they took long standing jumps. They seemed able to stop suddenly on the tips of their toes and give the ball a wicked flick that took it from right in front of an opposition player. They seemed to float upon the field as if they were walking on air.

By the time the score reached 4–4, Mr Gregory was clenching his fists. But by now his team were too shaken and bewildered to change their tactics. They settled for massing back in defence, and in the later part of the second half the ball hardly crossed the centre-line.

Piano Legs Cooper, a lone spectator, leaned against the goalpost and watched the activity at the other end of the field.

The final goal came from a free kick. The Stapleton captain had handled the ball during a particularly tight struggle for possession. Sarvindar took it and simply tapped it across to Billy at his left. Billy took aim through a gap in the opposition line but the keeper reached it and thrust it to the side. A corner.

Bayram went to take the kick, while

Sarvindar gave hasty instructions. As the ball travelled into the air, three Skimpole Street players suddenly moved three or four steps back into the field. Startled, their Stapleton Road defenders turned to watch. In the moment when they weren't looking, Billy took the ball, and shot it to Sarvindar who sent it rolling across the line even as the goalie dived for it.

The next disturbance had everyone gaping. A loud hooting noise was heard, and as they looked off the field, a red double-decker bus came trundling in and stopped in the car park. From behind the big windscreen, a figure was waving in triumph.

"She's done it!" shouted Mr Sandford.

"She's passed!" shouted Gary.

Skimpole Street School's Chief

Trainer came running from the cab of her bus to join the little group at the sideline.

The referee had waved the game on, and the green and yellow of Skimpole Street again hemmed in the blue and white stripes of the defenders. Stapleton Road, champions of the

Inter-Schools Football Competition, were not going to give in. They battled on to the end, and when the final whistle blew, the score remained at 5–4.

"Well, Mr Watkins, your lads made a remarkable recovery in the second half," said Mr Gregory. "Mr Archer, the referee, tells me that he has never seen a school team play such an artistic game. I must admit, I had my doubts at first, but all things considered, I am sure that Skimpole Street School should be re-admitted to the Inter-Schools League. And if I take that view, I think you can be confident that no one will disagree."

"I'm sure they won't, quite sure, Mr Gregory," said Mr Watkins happily.

That evening, Mr Sandford cooked an Admiral's Feast, something he did only on the most extra-special occasions. It began with buttered shrimps on toast, followed by a magnificent fish pie, topped with golden-brown mashed potato, and served with cabbage, carrots, mushrooms, peas, and grilled tomatoes. For pudding there was a vast bowl of trifle. Its smooth creamy surface had been decorated with hundreds and thousands, in the form of two numbers: 5–4.

Billy Gray and his mother had been invited to join the feast.

"I don't know when I've been so excited," said Mrs Gray. "I didn't take any interest when Billy played football before. In fact, I tried to put him off. I didn't know it could be so thrilling."

"Football's a funny game, isn't it? But this is just the beginning," said Mrs Sandford.

Billy and Gary grinned at each other. Today was enough for them. The future could wait.

Harriet Castor
Milly of the Rovers

Illustrated by Christyan Fox

For the old Regent's Park mid-week mixed team –
and for J. B., the best footballer I know

1. Sal's Salon

SWOOOOSH!

The ball whizzed through the air and landed at Milly's feet. YEARRGGH! went the crowd, thumping the air in approval.

"And Milly Hawkins is on the ball, Jeff. She's making a run for it down the left wing."

"Just look at her go, Dave! The best striker in the world today – what a pleasure to watch!"

"Yes, Jeff, and what a run this is! A dummy, a swerve, and the Brazilian defence is all over the place."

"They won't be happy with this one, Dave. The goalkeeper's off his line . . . but Hawkins has bamboozled him and –"

"GOAL!!!!!!"

"In-cred-ible!"

All around the stadium, thousands of voices started chanting:

"MIL-LY! MIL-LY! MIL-LY!"

"Milly! *Milly!*"

A familiar voice broke into Milly's dream.

"What are you doing to Mrs Fotherington-Smythe's hair?"

"Oops."

Milly's mother snatched away the comb and hairdryer. She looked very cross.

"Honestly, my girl, you'll never make a good hairdresser if you can't concentrate. Fetch the broom and sweep up the clippings."

"Sorry, Mum."

It was a Friday after school and Milly was helping out at her mother's salon.

She was supposed to be learning how to be a hairdresser, but all Milly really wanted to do was play football.

"Stupid game," her mother always said when Milly told her. "It's a waste of time."

The shop was called Sal's Salon. This wasn't after Milly's mother – her name was Jennifer. Milly didn't know who 'Sal' was.

Sal's Salon had pink peeling wallpaper and big pink chairs that you could pump up and down with a foot pedal. It was quite fun. But it wasn't a patch on a game of –

"Broom!" said Milly's mother.

"Right-ho," said Milly, and went to get it.

She tried very hard to concentrate on

what she was doing.

She even tried listening in to Mrs Fotherington-Smythe's conversation –

". . . new Council Leader, Dr Pinch . . . blah, blah, blah . . . she's a real new broom, Horace says . . . blah, blah, blah . . . has a bee in her bonnet . . ."

– but it was so boring.

". . . about making this town a success . . . going to shut down any hospitals, shops or schools that aren't glamorous enough, she says . . . You'd better watch out yourself, Jennifer – she'll be checking up on Sal's Salon, too."

Milly's mum laughed nervously. But Milly didn't notice. In her head, she was already back at Wembley.

2. Milly's Left Foot

What Milly's mother didn't realize was that although Milly looked like an ordinary girl – she wasn't one.

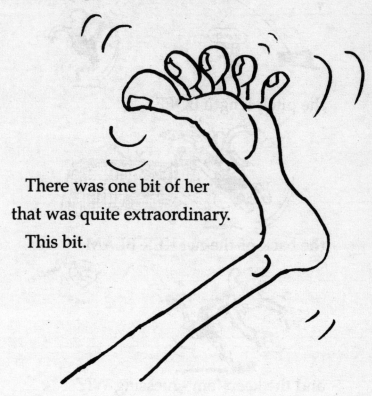

There was one bit of her that was quite extraordinary. This bit.

Milly's left foot was amazing. It was the best footballing foot in the whole of Grimethorpe Combined School, capable of things other feet could only dream of.

Things like

the pitch-length BOFF

the back-of-the-net KER-BLAM

and the keep-'em'-guessing WIZ-

FIDDLE.

Sadly, Milly's right foot wasn't so good. In fact, when it came to kicking a ball, Milly's right foot was the wrong foot. It was about as useful as a piece of fudge.

This wouldn't have been a problem, except that Milly couldn't tell left from right. There she'd be, in the middle of a match, on-line for scoring the best goal of the season – she'd take a swing . . .

. . . and the ball would dribble off in completely the wrong direction.

"Bother!"

It was very frustrating.

But Milly was going to be a footballing legend, of that she was absolutely certain.

Foot-ball...
Leg-end...
Get it?

And one day, somehow, she and her school team, Grimethorpe Rovers, were going to be heroes. That would stop her mum calling football a waste of time!

There was just one problem. Grimethorpe Rovers never won anything.

They were quite possibly the worst football team in history, and they were the laughing stock of Grimethorpe Combined School.

Even Milly had to admit that the line-up wasn't promising:

There were the triplets, Shaz, Kaz and Maz. They always insisted on running everywhere together. Which wouldn't have been a problem, except that they always ran AWAY from the ball.

People ...... can't tell ...... us apart...

There was Duncan
from Class 2, who was
brilliant at dribbling
. . . just not the sort you
do with your feet.

There was Polly, who couldn't see
where the other players were, let alone
the ball . . .

and Alan, the
goalie, who was
keen – but on
gymnastics,
not football.

Then there was
Colin, who was
allergic to everything,

Trevor, who could
trip himself up without
help from anyone else,

..oops!

BOING!

Cress, who was very
talented with
chewing-gum – but
not with a football,

and Nigel, who always fell asleep at
matches – even when he was on the ball.

Last but not least, there was the captain:
Milly herself. Just last Saturday she'd
been racing towards goal at a million
miles an hour . . .

She'd got past
one tackle,

two tackles,

three tackles,

and when the coast was clear, and she'd
sorted out (for once) which foot was
which –

POW! – she'd slammed the ball into the
back of the net.

It was only when she'd been halfway
through her Darren Dangerfoot victory

knee-slide that she'd realized it was actually the wrong net . . . and it was her own team who'd been trying to stop her.

"Milly!"

"Sorry."

No – if Milly's mum, and the rest of the world, were ever going to take Grimethorpe Rovers seriously, they were going to have to shape up.

But how?

3. A Problem for Mr Bute

Brrriiinnnggg!

That same Friday night, the phone rang in the office of Mr Bute, the headmaster of Grimethorpe Combined.

"Hello?" he said, picking up the receiver.

"Bute?" snapped a voice. "It's Pinch here. Dr Pinch – the new Council Leader."

"Oh, how nice -" began Mr Bute.

"I've just got one thing to say to you, Bute," Dr Pinch interrupted. "And that's: SUCCESS."

"S-success?" stammered Mr Bute, feeling rather flustered.

"That's what I said," replied Dr Pinch. "There's no room for failures in this town. It's new Council policy. If anything's a failure, we'll get rid of it. And of all the failures I can see around here –" (she frowned at her secretary, who went scurrying out of the room) "– of all the failures I can see around here, Bute, Grimethorpe Combined is the biggest."

Dr Pinch swung her chair round to face the massive wall-map pinned up behind her, and jabbed at it with her pointer as she talked.

"There are two schools in this town," she explained, as though Mr Bute didn't know already. "Grimethorpe and Redlands. This town isn't big enough for two schools. It doesn't need two schools. It's wasteful. It's greedy. It's lax and lardy. It's uneconomical. One of them must go. And it's my job to decide which one."

Mr Bute gulped. If it was Grimethorpe versus Redlands, Grimethorpe wouldn't stand a chance.

"Streamlined. Sleek. Smart. These are words we like, Bute. But these are not words we can use to describe Grimethorpe Combined, now, can we?"

Mr Bute, slumped in his chair, surveyed his office miserably. No – the sagging beanbags, the scatter-cushions, the pictures of Mrs Bute and little Ruby – none of them were what you might call streamlined. Or smart.

Dr Pinch was still talking. "A fortnight, Bute. That's what you have. Two weeks. Fourteen days. Three hundred and thirty-six hours. And then there will be a meeting of the Council's new 'One School' committee, which I've just set up –" (actually she'd only just thought of it) "– and we will be deciding which school stays open and which school shuts down. In the meantime, my inspectors will be coming round to investigate."

213

Mr Bute heard her ring off. He stared into space for several seconds, listening to the dialling tone. Then he slowly replaced the receiver.

Just five minutes ago, he'd been a happy man. He'd been about to go home to a lovely comfy evening with his family, looking forward to the next week at his comfy, happy school. And now . . . now he felt like one of his beanbags. He had lost his stuffing.

He got out of his chair and reached for his coat. He'd have to find another job. He couldn't work for that awful headmaster, Mr Slimjim, at Redlands – it didn't bear thinking about. No, he'd have to give up teaching altogether.

And Mr Bute, who never usually felt the cold, pulled his overcoat tightly around him, and shivered as he made his way out into the night.

4. Just Another Match

The next day, Grimethorpe Rovers had
their last but one match of the season. It
was against Ruffemup United, a team in
the next town.

As usual, the Rovers went there in the
team bus, a rusty old contraption held
together by three bootlaces and a
skipping-rope. It had red plastic seats that
stuck to your legs on hot days, and it
smelt unmistakably of DOG.

The dog in question was called Punter.
He belonged to Mr Beagley, the school
caretaker and bus driver. Punter looked
something like a cross between an old
bathmat and a dish mop, and he smelt
like he'd been rolling in oily puddles for
several days. Which he probably had.

But, despite being the smelliest, hairiest

dog in the world, Punter was also the Rovers' best, most loyal and ONLY supporter.

You could spot him on the touchline at every single Grimethorpe match and you could spot his hairs at every match all over the Grimethorpe kit.

Today was no different. In fact it was, altogether, quite a usual sort of Saturday.

Alan the goalie spent his time practising handstands against the cross-bar.

Colin went for a header and found he was allergic to the ball. And Milly forgot to change direction after half-time and scored another own-goal.

Ruffemup United were all little squits, but they were as hard as nails and liked proving it.

They got fifteen goals.

Grimethorpe Rovers got none. But they did get

three grazed knees

five bruised ankles

one black eye

and a new-look strip.
Yep, thought Milly as the bus spluttered
homewards. Just a usual sort of Saturday.

5. SUCCESS

On Monday morning, Mr Bute went to
assembly with a heavy heart. As soon as
the Grimethorpe pupils saw him, they
knew that something was wrong. Usually
he sat on the edge of the stage, swinging
his legs and cracking jokes. But this
morning he stood up, ramrod straight,
and tried very hard to look stern. He gave
a long talk about doing your best, and
polishing your shoes and being
streamlined (whatever that meant), and

he held up a big notice
with SUCCESS
written on it. But
you could tell his
heart wasn't in it;
he'd spelt it wrong.

"It's no use," he said at last. "We're done for."

"What do you mean, Mr B?" piped up Shona McVale, who was in Milly's class. Shona was going to be a reporter – the sort who interviews the big stars. For now, though, Shona was making do with running the school magazine, the *Grimethorpe Times*.

"Well, Shona, it's like this –" began Mr Bute. And he told her all about Dr Pinch's plans to shut down one of the town's schools.

And about how the inspectors were going to come round to measure which school was the most successful.

And about how, if Grimethorpe was

shut down, all the Grimethorpe pupils
would have to go to Redlands instead.

And, at this, some of the infants turned
pale and started crying, and the juniors
reached for their catapults and their
super-ballistic homemade pea–shooters.

To have to go to Redlands – it was a fate

worse than . . . well, than compulsory Cheese Pie for school dinner every day for a whole year.

Why was it so bad? You just had to take a look at the Redlanders to see why.

They had a sharp, cut-and-thrust look in their eyes, and a proud tilt to their noses. Their shoelaces were ironed, their hair was polished, and they could recite the thirteen times table backwards at the drop of a hat.

They were also the meanest, cheatingest, break-every-rule skunks in the world. But just because they

always looked squeaky clean and lickety-
split tidy, the people in Milly's town
always said:

Ah, Redlands pupils. They're so well-behaved, don't you think so, Dorothy?

Ooh, yes!

While, even though Grimethorpers
were the bravest, most fearless, against-
all-the-odds good guys 'n' gals in the
world, the townsfolk said:

Good for nothing, that Grimethorpe rabble. They really spoil the atmosphere.

They do.

Everything bad that Redlanders did, Grimethorpers got blamed for it. No wonder they hated each other.

"There's nothing else for it," said Mr Bute, looking round the hall. "We'll just have to try our best to be the most successful school."

And try their best they certainly did.

All that day, Grimethorpe pupils were busy polishing, cleaning and sprucing. Cushions were plumped, sofas were swept, and cracks were hidden behind brand new posters. Even Punter was given a bath – though he went straight back to his favourite oily puddle afterwards.

By the time Dr Pinch's inspectors – Inspector Slicer, Inspector Nettle and Inspector Trim – turned up the next morning, Grimethorpe Combined School had taken on a new lease of life.

And that included the pupils, too. They'd polished their satchels and pulled up their socks, and whenever an inspector was nearby, they made sure they talked loudly about very complicated long division sums.

Even Mr Bute made a special effort to wear shirts and ties that didn't clash. He found it rather tricky.

6. Dr Pinch has a Plan

All week, the inspectors at Grimethorpe and the inspectors at Redlands ticked and crossed, and measured and weighed, and sniffed the air for the scent of success.

By Friday, Dr Pinch was not pleased. Worse than that – Dr Pinch was furious. Because somehow – and how she didn't quite know – Grimethorpe and Redlands had got equal points. They were neck and neck.

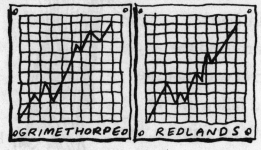

Now, despite what she'd said to Mr Bute, Dr Pinch wasn't truly interested in finding out which school she should close – she'd already decided. Whatever the inspectors' reports said, Dr Pinch wanted to shut down Grimethorpe Combined.

She didn't like Grimethorpe. It was a comfy, happy place, and comfiness and happiness were two of the things that Dr Pinch hated most of all.

But there was another
reason, too – one that
no one else knew
about. It was a secret
locked away in Dr
Pinch's rather
cold, hard
heart. And the
secret was that she
had fallen in love
with Mr Slimjim, the
Redlands
headmaster.

So if – she shuddered to think of it – if
Grimethorpe actually won the contest and
she had to shut down Redlands, it would
be a disaster! Her Slimjim – in disgrace!

No – Redlands had to win. And Dr
Pinch had to find some way to make sure
that they did.

So she came up with a plan.

Dr Pinch's plan came to her late that
night when she was lying in the bath, and
she thought it was a particularly brilliant

231

one. It was this: since the scores were level, there would have to be a tie-break. And, to make completely sure that Redlands would win it, she had decided that the tie-break should be a football match. Or, more precisely, should be the Grudge Cup match that was due to be played the next Saturday.

The Grudge Cup was a once-a-year football match between Grimethorpe Rovers and Dynamo Redlands. It was the last match of the season and, for the Rovers, it was the worst.

In all the fifty-three years since the Grudge Cup had been invented, Grimethorpe had won it just once. That was the year there was a freak storm at half-time and all the Redlands players were struck by lightning.

Every other year, the Rovers hadn't stood a chance.

"Excellent!" thought Dr Pinch to herself. "My darling Slimjim's school will have no problem beating that bunch of losers."

7. The Challenge

The next day, Mr Bute had another phone
call from Dr Pinch, telling him about the
tie-break. As soon as he had put the
phone down, he pressed the button on his
intercom.

"Miss Marchmount?" he said into the
speaker. "Miss Marchmount – please
bring me Milly Hawkins from Class 3. I
need to speak to her urgently."

A second later Miss Marchmount,
carried at lightning speed by her new
SpringStep training shoes, had reached
Class 3 – just at the moment when Milly
had mixed up the test tube in her right
hand with the test tube in her left hand,
and had managed to make the world's
first double choc-chip stink bomb

explode. It was lucky that none of the
inspectors were observing Class 3's
science lesson that morning.

"Milly," said Miss Marchmount, wiping burnt hundreds and thousands off her glasses, "Mr Bute needs to see you straightaway."

"Right-ho," said Milly.

Mr Bute decided not to ask why Milly looked like a large hot fudge sundae. He got on with what he had to say.

He explained about the tie-break. And how the Rovers were going to have to win the Grudge Cup.

"Win?" said Milly. "*Win?* You mean actually get more goals than Dynamo Redlands?"

"I'm afraid so," said Mr Bute.

"But . . . but . . ." Milly spluttered. The Dynamo Redlands players were the biggest, meanest bruisers in the footballing universe. Playing against them was like getting run over by a steamroller. And what's more, though their playing was dirty, just because their kit was clean the ref never seemed to notice.

Now, if Mr Bute had asked Grimethorpe Rovers to beat Brazil, or AC Milan, it mightn't have been so bad . . . but Dynamo Redlands? It was impossible.

"Have we got time to buy in players from anywhere else?" asked Milly, thinking of those big transfer deals she was always hearing about on the telly. "Like Manchester United, or Arsenal, or – or Liverpool?"

Mr Bute smiled sadly. "I don't think so," he said. "We'll just have to make do with what we've got."

Milly swallowed. Mr Bute was looking at her earnestly. Footballing legends, Milly reminded herself, don't bottle out.

"We'll give it a go, Mr Bute," she said firmly. Then she fainted.

8. Inspiration

At break, Milly went to talk to Punter. She
found him round the back of Mr
Beagley's office (which was actually a
shed), playing dead lions.

238

"What am I going to do, Punter?" she asked him, staring deep into the fluff and wondering where his eyes were.

Punter slurped her on the nose. It wasn't much help.

The fact was, Milly had already tried everything she could think of to make Grimethorpe Rovers into a lean, mean fighting machine.

She'd tried training sessions.

There'd been the early morning runs that only she and Punter had turned up to.

Then there'd been the early morning runs that even Punter hadn't turned up to.

Then there'd
been that
exercise session.
At the next
match, everyone
had been so stiff
they'd hardly been able to move at all.

She'd tried tactics, too. She'd come up
with all sorts of clever plans, and drawn
them out in complicated diagrams. But at
the team talk before the next match she'd
ended up, as usual, having to explain the
rules of the game to some of the players
who'd forgotten since last week.

And the one time they'd tried out
different formations on the pitch it'd
looked more like *Come Dancing* than
Match of the Day.

It was no use. Milly had run out of
ideas. Just when the Rovers – and
Grimethorpe – needed her most.

She ruffled Punter's fluff and went
sadly back into school. Her mother was
right – perhaps she'd have to be a
hairdresser after all.

But then that night, Milly had a strange
dream.

She was back in Mr Bute's office. But
instead of Mr Bute sitting behind the
desk, there was Milly's footballing
hero, Darren Dangerfoot. And he was
saying one thing to her, over and over
again.

"We'll have to make do with what
we've got. We'll have to . . ."

Milly woke up with a start. "A-ha!" she said out loud.

She had just had the most wonderful idea.

9. Secret Weapons

The next day, strange things started
happening at Grimethorpe Combined
School. Odd noises were heard coming
from behind Mr Beagley's shed.

Milly was seen running around with a
very large roll of sticky-tape.

And Nigel was several times spotted
almost awake, even in lessons.

It was all very mysterious. The Rovers
were in training, but this wasn't the sort
of training anyone had ever seen before.

And quite what it had to do with a
game of football, nobody was sure.

"It's no use hoping we'll all turn into
Darren Dangerfoot," said Milly when
Shona asked her for a pre-match
interview. "But we've each got talents –

CLICK!
CLICK!

and we're going to use them. No further comment."

Even Shona was confused.

"Talents?"

The day before the big match, Milly ran straight home from school to practise in the back yard.

She'd perfected the new Hawkins Hustle, and her beat-the-best-goalie-in-the-world banana shot wasn't bad either.

Milly had just hit the ball perfectly for the three hundred and ninety-eighth time, when her mother called her in.

Milly! Come here a minute!

Milly's mum was sitting at the kitchen table. She had a letter in one hand, and her piggy bank in the other. She was looking very worried.

"Milly," she said, "I need you to work in the salon tomorrow."

Milly felt her smile crumble. "But Mum!" she cried. "Tomorrow's Saturday!"

"Exactly," said her mother. "So you won't have to miss school."

"No, no – I mean, tomorrow's the Grudge Cup," said Milly frantically.

"I can't miss it. The Rovers have got to win or they'll shut down Grimethorpe. Dr Pinch says so."

Milly's mother sighed. "Well, Dr Pinch has some other things to say as well," she said. And she handed Milly the letter.

"Dear Mrs Hawkins . . ." Dr Pinch had written. "Sal's Salon is a disgrace to the town. It looks a mess. It ought to be shut down. I'll give you until Tuesday to spruce it up – or else you can shut it up. No buts. My word is final. Yours, Dr Prudence Pinch, Council Leader."

"What will you do?" asked Milly.

Her mother shook her head in despair. "I just haven't got enough money to do up the salon – and I can't see how I can get it before Tuesday. Unless – if you work tomorrow, Milly, I can have more customers in, and we might just make enough. It's our only hope."

Milly didn't know what to say.

"If Dr Pinch shuts the salon," her mum went on, "I won't have a job – and I don't know if I'll be able to get another one. At least if Grimethorpe shuts you could go to Redlands."

Milly opened her mouth to say 'Yeuch!',
but then she shut it again. She didn't have
a choice. She was going to have to miss
the match.

10. Grudge Cup Blues

The next morning, Milly was up early, combing and drying, washing and sweeping. But all she could think of was the match.

Nine o'clock – three hours to go before kick-off . . .

two hours to go . . .

one hour . . .

half an hour . . .

It was too much to bear.

Mrs Fotherington-Smythe was in again, and Milly was put in charge of her curlers.

... Horace .. blah, blah, blah... golf club ... blah, blah, blah...

Milly couldn't stand it anymore. She had to do something.

Without stopping to think, she clamped

Mrs Fotherington-Smythe into the big drier, and set it for forty-five minutes each way.

Then she said one last "Yes, Mrs Fotherington-Smythe. How interesting, Mrs Fotherington-Smythe," and slipped out of the back door.

Meanwhile, at the Grimethorpe football pitch, the Dynamo Redlands bus had just glided into view, twinkling in the sunshine. It wasn't much like the Rovers' bus. It had plushy seats and air conditioning, and the name of the local supermarket in glossy letters all down the side. The faces at the window had a cut-and-thrust look in their eyes, and a proud tilt to their noses. Their kit was silky and dog-hair-free.

The bus pulled to a halt, and autograph-hunters crowded round. Out strolled the team, looking relaxed and confident.

Amongst them were . . .

Larry Ginnyka, local hero, and captain of Dynamo Redlands, Mary-Donna, their fiendishly good (and unscrupulous) striker, and Vinny Terribles, the Redlands bully-boy, who specialized in kicking you when the ref wasn't looking.

The Grimethorpe players were already warming up.

But where was Milly? The ref was starting to look edgy.

"We'll have to start without her."

He put the ball on the centre line, tossed
a coin to decide who should kick it first
and put his whistle in his mouth.

Just then . . .

Milly had just made it. The ref blew his whistle, and the match began.

It was tough.

It was muddy.

It was mean.

But by half-time, Dynamo Redlands were worried. This wasn't the Grimethorpe Rovers they knew. If it hadn't been for the tell-tale dog hairs, no one would have recognized Milly and her gang.

The triplets, Shaz, Kaz and Maz, still went everywhere together, but now they had learnt to charge, screaming a blood-curdling war-cry as they went.

Polly was armed with a magnifying glass taped to each lens of her specs giving her SUPER HAWK VISION. The Redlands players didn't know what to do now she wasn't giving them the ball all the time.

In goal, Alan had started putting his best gymnastic skills to good use.

Trevor hadn't stopped tripping over but he HAD learnt to take Vinny Terribles down with him when he fell.

The score so far was 0-0. The Redlands team were rattled. They were used to being at least 9-0 up by now. Something had to be done. The players huddled close together as they sucked on their oranges.

Then the whistle blew for the second half.

It was tougher.

It was muddier.

It was meaner.

But still the Rovers were holding out.

Then Milly noticed Mary-Donna wink
at Vinny, and not in a very nice way.

A few moments later, as soon as the
ref's back was turned, Vinny went for

Trevor, and sent him crashing to the
ground.

"That's what you get for messing with
me, loser."

"Tripped over his own feet, as usual,"
said the ref.

Trevor had to be taken off the field.

"We've had it now!" thought Milly. "It's
eleven against ten. We've no chance."

No wonder Redlands were suddenly
looking happier.

But just then, Milly saw something
running on to the pitch. It was Punter!

"A dog as a substitute?" Milly
shrugged. "It's got to be better than
nothing."

There were only a few minutes of the
match to go. The score was still 0-0.

"If we can just hang on a bit longer,"
thought Milly desperately.

Then, all of a sudden, she spied Punter

with the ball. He was moving faster than
she'd ever seen him move in her life.

First he pushed the ball to
Duncan's feet . . .

SLOOP!!

. . . then he set off with it along the
pitch.

"He won't get far," thought Milly,
seeing the Redlands players running up
to tackle from all sides. But suddenly they
stopped, holding their noses.

Milly gave a yelp of laughter. Beaten by
the Punter smell!

Punter steadily made his way down the whole field. Milly realized he was heading her way. She got herself into position in front of the goal. Mr Beagley was holding up a sign for

her, so she knew it was the right one.

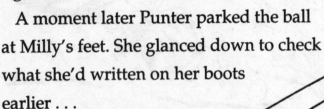

A moment later Punter parked the ball at Milly's feet. She glanced down to check what she'd written on her boots earlier . . .

. . . took a swing, and – POW! – thwacked the ball as hard as she could. It did a perfect banana curve.

The Redlands goalie dived, but, slippery with Duncan's dribble, the ball shot straight through his fingers and landed firmly in the back of the net.

"GOAL!!!!!"

The noise almost drowned out the referee's final whistle.

Milly stood there, her eyes as big as dinner plates and her mouth stretched into the widest grin ever.

1-0! They'd won!

Then suddenly it was mayhem. Grimethorpe pupils were running on to

the pitch, hugging every Rover in sight.
Some even forgot the smell and hugged
Punter. Milly found herself lifted up on to
the players' shoulders and paraded
around like a star.

Grimethorpe was saved! And the
Rovers were footballing heroes – they'd
never be laughed at again!

Meanwhile the Redlanders were
wailing and gnashing their teeth. Now
Redlands would be shut down and they'd
have to go to Grimethorpe. It was a fate
worse than . . . well, worse than
compulsory Cheese Pie for school dinners
for a whole year.

Suddenly, a voice cut through all the
noise.

"Milly Hawkins! Come here at once!
What did you mean by sneaking off like
that? Just look what's happened to Mrs
Fotherington-Smythe's hair!"

It was Milly's mum. And she didn't look pleased.

Milly couldn't help it. She tried very hard not to. But when she opened her mouth to apologize, all that came out was:

"Ha, ha, ha, ha!"

"How can you laugh?" said her mother. "Now we'll have to give Mrs Fotherington-Smythe a refund, and we'll never have enough money by Tuesday. Dr Pinch will shut us down!"

11. Sal's Salon Again

But it didn't come to that. Because the next day, the newspapers reported that straight after the match, Dr Pinch and Mr Slimjim had disappeared together. Someone said they'd run off to get married. But no one found out for certain – because they never came back.

So there was an election for a new Council Leader.

And the winner was Mr Bute.

And Mr Bute declared that he would cancel all Dr Pinch's orders. Everything that she'd been about to shut down, could stay open – and never mind if it didn't look streamlined. Or smart.

Even Redlands should stay open, said Mr Bute. (To be honest, he didn't fancy

having the Redlands pupils in his classes.)
But he appointed a new head for
Redlands, the Reverend Daisychain, who
wasn't like Mr Slimjim at all.

REV. DAISYCHAIN

"This is all thanks to Milly," announced
Mr Bute proudly at assembly the next
week. "And I've been trying to think
what present we could give her as a
reward. Tell me, Milly, what would you
like?"

"Well, there is one thing I can think of,"

said Milly, "but everyone will need to help."

So the next weekend, all the pupils and teachers of Grimethorpe Combined brought ladders and brushes and pots of paint to Sal's Salon. And by Monday morning, it was the shiniest, smartest salon in town.

New customers flocked to see it. Milly's mother had never been so busy.

Soon she had enough money to pay for a proper assistant, called Gerald.

"No, I don't need any help today, Milly," she said each week. "Anyway, haven't you got a football match to go to?"

And, when she had the time, Milly's mum even came to see a few of them.

But, even though Sal's Salon became the most popular place in town, one customer stayed away.

Milly's mother even offered her free haircuts for a year. But it was no use. Mrs Fotherington-Smythe never darkened the door of Sal's Salon again.

ly Reporter

'ALL THE WORLD'S A FOOTBALL"

Says Milly Hawkins: Footballing Legend.

A happy Milly Hawkins with the Grudge Cup

Grimethorpe Rovers are justly celebrating a 1-0 victory over Dynamo Redlands. 9 year-old Milly Hawkins, Grimethorpes centre forward said she was "over the moon with the result. In a game of two halves Grimethorpe achieved the right result on the

disappeared before the end of the game was said to be as sick as a parrot. Mr.Bute the